Clancy's Coat

Clancy's

FREDERICK WARNE · NEW YORK LONDON

Coat BY Eve Bunting

ILLUSTRATIONS BY Lorinda Bryan Cauley

Frederick Warne & Co., Inc.   New York, New York

LIBRARY OF CONGRESS CATALOGING IN PUBLICATION DATA
Bunting, Eve, 1928–
Clancy's coat.
SUMMARY: Although Tippitt the tailor has
trouble getting around to returning farmer Clancy's
old winter coat, he is quicker to take advantage of the
opportunity to mend a broken friendship.
[1. Coats—Fiction.   2. Tailors—Fiction.
3. Friendship—Fiction]
I. Cauley, Lorinda Bryan, ill.   II Title.
PZ7.B91527Ck   1983   [Fic]   83-6575
ISBN O-7232-6252-7

1 2 3 4 5 88 87 86 85 84

BOOK DESIGN BY BARBARA DU PREE KNOWLES

PRINTED IN THE U.S.A. BY HOLYOKE LITHOGRAPH CO.

Again for Mary Sullivan . . .
who put me on the trail
of *Clancy's Coat*.   —E.B.

To the memory of
Thomas H. Cauley.   —L.B.C.

Tippitt the tailor was having his morning tea when he looked out the window and saw Clancy coming along the road.

"Well, I'll be jakered," he said to Sam, his sheepdog. Hadn't old Clancy sworn never to look in Tippitt's direction again? Hadn't he insulted Tippitt, and Tippitt's good cow, Bridget, too, just because Bridget forgot her manners one day and got into Clancy's vegetable garden?

"Here comes trouble, Sam," Tippitt said, shading his eyes from the sun. "We'll wait for it at the door, for there's no sense inviting trouble into your house."

It wasn't till Clancy got closer that Tippitt saw he was carrying a parcel.

"I've brought you work to do," Clancy said, stopping
in front of them. "And I've brought it for the
reason that you're the best tailor in Crossgar, and not
for the sake of old friendships. Though we were the
best of friends and the best of neighbors once, in the
days before your cow destroyed my garden."

Tippitt stepped aside and so did Sam. "If it's work you need done you'd better come in."

"I'll come in, then, but I'll not be staying."

"And who asked you to stay?" Tippitt pushed away the teapot and made room on the table for the parcel.

Clancy undid the string and pulled out an old, black coat, shiny with time and wear. Sam cringed back from the smell of mothballs.

"There's a lot of use left in this old coat," Clancy said. "It was a fine piece of cloth and it just needs turning." He pulled one of the sleeves out to show the red wool lining.

"What I need is for you to make the inside be the outside and the outside be the inside, if you get my meaning."

Tippitt raised his eyebrows. "Surely. The coat needs turning."

"That's it." Clancy hung it on the back of a chair and rubbed his hands together. "Powerful cold out." He eyed the brown teapot with the steam rising from its spout.

Tippitt made no move to take another mug from
the dresser. "You said you wouldn't be staying."

"Right," Clancy said. "When will the coat be ready?"

"By Saturday."

"I'll be here for it."

Tippitt and Sam watched Clancy go. "It was a sorry day when Bridget got in his vegetables," Tippitt said. "He's a great man for his growing things. It comes from having neither chick nor child to call his own."

Sam nodded, the way he always did when Tippitt talked to him.

"Though my own children's grown and my wife is
gone I still have you, my good cow, and my wee hen.
All he has are his cabbages and turnips. It's not much,
when all's said and done."

Sam nodded again and Tippitt examined the coat.
"It'll be as easy to do as skimming cream," he said.
"And it'll be done for Saturday."

It would have been, too, except that the night was extra cold, and in the middle of it Tippitt heard Bridget mooing in the barn. When he got up and looked for something to put round her to keep her warm, there was Clancy's coat. Tippitt took it out, spread it over the cow, and forgot all about it till the next Saturday when he was having dinner and looked out to see Clancy heading up the road.

"Jakers!" Tippitt said to Sam. "Didn't I forget
all about Clancy's coat! We'd better invite him to
stay a while this time, for he'll be powerful annoyed
and in need of soothing."

"Come in, come in," he called from the open door
as Sam nodded and wagged his tail.

Clancy took off his muffler and set it on the dresser.

"I see you're eating your dinner," he said. "I'll not keep you, for I only came for my old coat."

"It's not ready yet," Tippitt said. "It's been over my . . . over . . . overlooked. But . . ."

"Moo . . . oooo!" Bridget called from the barn.

"I'll have it for you for certain sure by next Saturday," Tippitt said quickly. "Would you have a cup of tea before you go?" He poured it from the pot, thick as tar and black as night.

"You always did make a good cup of tea." Clancy sat down at the table and eyed the remains of Tippitt's dinner. "Watery looking potatoes you have there. I'm thinking you bought those from O'Donnell of the Glen?"

"Aye," Tippitt said. "And they're like candle grease."

Clancy finished his tea and stood up. "I'll be back for the coat on Saturday."

When he opened the door the March wind came in, cold as a stepmother's breath. "I'll be glad of that old coat," Clancy said, winding his muffler tight round his neck. "There's a lot of use in it yet."

Sam and Tippitt watched till he got all the way to his own wee house down the road, and then Tippitt went to the barn and got the coat from where Bridget was lying on it. And a hard job she made of it, for she didn't want to give it up.

Tippitt shook the hairs from it and set it next to his
sewing machine. "I'll start on you in the morning," he
told it. And he would have.

Only, that night the wind came up with a terrible fierceness and it blew the whole back window out of Tippitt's house, waking him from a sound sleep. In his hurry to find something to keep out the cold Tippitt saw the coat. He tacked it up where the glass had been and forgot all about it.

The next Saturday Clancy knocked at the door.

"Jakers save us!" Tippitt told Sam. "And the coat's not ready yet! This will take some quick thinking."

He pulled the best chair close to the fire and plumped out the cushions, and he and Sam were both smiling as they met Clancy at the door.

"Come in, sit down," Tippitt invited. "The coat's not fixed yet. It's been in my . . . in my . . . in my mind since I saw you last. But it'll be done by next Saturday for certain sure."

Tippitt noticed that Clancy had a sack slung over his shoulder. "What's this?" he asked.

"Potatoes," Clancy said. "I have them going to waste and I can't stand to see anybody eating poison like the ones you were eating last week. Not even you, Tippitt."

"Well, I'm much obliged." Tippitt decided to ignore the last part of the speech. "Will you have a cup of tea and a piece of my fresh baked bread before you go?"

He sliced a piece, spread it with butter, and carried it to where Clancy had seated himself in the best chair with its plumped up cushions.

"You always did have the whitest bread and the sweetest butter," Clancy said. "I can't buy the likes of it anywhere."

"It's Bridget's good buttermilk that goes into the both of them," Tippitt told him, and wished he'd been quiet because mention of Bridget might remind Clancy and set him off on another uproar.

But Clancy only said: "It's the care you give her. It shows up in what she gives back. Same as me and my garden."

Jakers, Tippitt thought, here it comes. But no more came.

"Saturday, then," Clancy said as he was leaving and Tippitt and Sam both nodded.

As soon as he'd gone Tippitt got the coat from the back window and nailed a piece of wood in its place. He put the coat on top of his sewing machine. "Don't be going any place else," he scolded it. "I'm getting to you tomorrow."

And he would have. Except that the very next day he

remembered that he'd promised Rosie O'Brien her skirt
for the Friday dance, so he threw Clancy's coat into
the corner till he had time to get at it, and Mary,
his hen, came right in and set herself on it. And the
first thing Tippitt heard was her clucking and panting
and swishing her feathers to get herself comfortable
before laying her eggs.

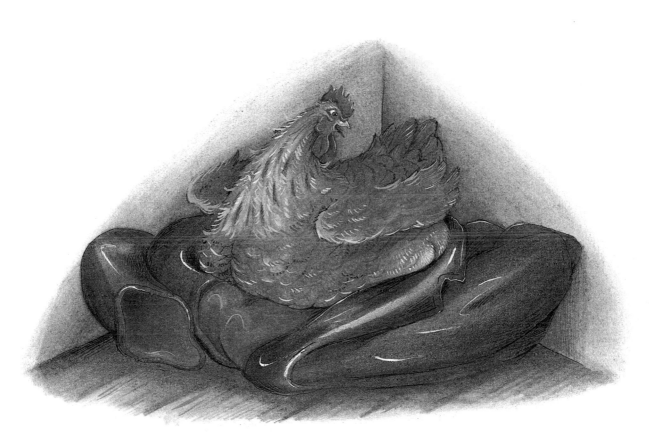

Tippitt scratched his head. "Jakers, Sam! It wouldn't
be decent to move Mary, and her in the middle of her
business. We'll just have to put Clancy off again and
we'll have to be smart about it."

On Saturday Tippitt moved his old sofa so that it hid
Mary and the coat. He wrapped a big square of yellow
butter and set it and a fresh brown loaf in the middle
of the table.

"Och, the coat's not finished yet, Clance," he said
when Clancy arrived and before he could ask.

"But there's good work being done on it, I'll promise
you that."

Then he pointed to the butter and the bread. "I've a couple of wee presents for you here."

"It's a long time since you called me 'Clance'," Clancy said gruffly. He set another sack on the table. "Here's a cabbage for you, and a bundle of leeks and carrots." His eyes slid away from Tippitt's and Tippitt knew he was wishing he'd never said 'garden' the week before just as Tippitt had wished he'd never said 'cow'.

They had tea together, sitting one on each side of the table, the fire flickering and the wee room as warm as toast. Tippitt asked about Clancy's bad leg and Clancy enquired about Tippitt's niece, the one who was married to a policeman and living in America.

"It's almost like old times," Clancy said as he got up to leave. "And I'll be back next week for the coat, for there's a lot of use left in it yet."

Mary rustled behind the sofa and went "Cluck, cluck."
"This time, by jakers, he'll have it," Tippitt told Sam
as soon as Clancy had gone. "Get a move on there with
your business, Mary."

When the chicks were hatched Tippitt gently moved
them and thanked Mary kindly for her trouble. Then
he carried the coat outside and spread it to air on the
hawthorne hedge.

But when he went to take it in he saw that a pair of sparrows were building a nest right in the middle of it.

Tippitt scratched his head. "Well, there's not a soul with a drop of kindness that would disturb a pair of lovebirds when they're building their nest. Should we tell Clance what's going on with his coat, or should we try putting him off another time? I'll admit to something, Sam. I like having Clance around again. And I noticed the way his hands touched those carrots and leeks he brought over. He loves them, so he does. I should have tried harder to know how he felt when poor Bridget stepped all over his garden."

Sam nodded.

"You think I should tell him where the coat is, then?"

Sam nodded again.

When Clancy came he brought a bunch of new rhubarb, pink and tender.

"Isn't that the loveliest thing?" Tippitt said. "And inside there's some of Bridget's good cream to go along with it, sweet as sugar and thick enough to walk on. Now . . . about your coat . . ."

"It's finished?" Clancy asked, and Tippitt thought he looked somehow disappointed.

"Not so you'd notice," he replied. He took Clancy out and showed him the sparrow's nest.

"Aye, it's spring," Clancy said. "The hedge is in blossom and the birds are building. Let them be, Tippitt. Sure I've no need of the coat till winter, now, and you'll have it done by then."

"You're a reasonable man, Clance," Tippitt said, and Sam nodded—twice.

"Not all the time," Clancy said. "But a man learns. A garden comes back with care and attention. I thought maybe a friendship could too."

Tippitt smiled and put his arm around Clancy's shoulders. "You're right," he said. "Now wasn't it the luckiest thing, Clance, that your old coat needed turning?"

Clancy winked. "I told you there was a lot of use left in it."

Tippitt chuckled. "Well, I'll be jakered!"